To Matthew, Christopher and John — J.D.

Text copyright © Jan Dean 1999
Illustrations copyright © Chris Mould 1999

First published in Great Britain in 1999
by Macdonald Young Books
an imprint of Wayland Publishers Ltd
61 Western Road
Hove
East Sussex
BN3 1JD

Find Macdonald Young Books on the internet at
http://www.myb.co.uk

The right of Jan Dean to be identified as the author
and Chris Mould as the illustrator of this Work has been
asserted by them in accordance with the
Copyright, Designs and Patents Act 1988

Designed by Don Martin
Printed and bound by Guernsey Press

British Library Cataloguing in Publication Data available

ISBN: 0 7500 2779 7

FROGSNOT ate my goldfish

JAN DEAN
Illustrated by Chris Mould

MACDONALD YOUNG BOOKS

Chapter One

My name is Cheesy Adams. I am tall and thin with hair like shredded wheat and I specialize in monsters. I didn't plan to be a monster specialist. Monsters are like splodgy inkblots all over your homework –
you don't plan them, you don't *want* them. But they burst into your life just the same. And they are *trouble*.

Luckily, I have an ace best friend – Zoom.
Monsters don't faze Zoom. I couldn't do without her.

Me and Zoom were walking home from Westerby Juniors, along Ryman Road. The houses are boarded up because the council is going to knock them down. I was showing Zoom my new water-squirter biro, when I dropped it – straight down a drain.

"Rats! That cost a bomb."

"We'll fish it out," Zoom announced. "I've got a crab-line at home. Wait here, I'll get it."

Zoom is the smallest person in our class, but she runs like lightning. She's also the bossiest. People do what Zoom says.

I sat on the kerb and waited. Ryman Road looked scarier now that I was alone. The empty houses looked spooky and to make matters worse strange noises came from the drain. It gurgled. Then it *groaned.* Nervously, I peered down the hole. It was very dark and hard to see, so I blinked, *and something blinked back.*

"Are you all right?" Zoom asked when she came back. "You look sort of… wobbly."

I pointed at the drain. My finger shook a bit. "There's something down there. I saw *eyes*, Zoom! Big, gloopy, shiny eyes. And there's a *smell.*"

She gave me a look. "It's a *drain*, Cheesy. Of course there's a smell."

"Not a drain smell. Something else."

But she wasn't listening. She was staring at the line. It was disappearing at top speed. She held on tight and yanked. "Gotcha!" she said.

"Phlergh! Humph! Skredge it!"

"What was that?"

I shook my head. My heart beat so fast, it felt like a frog jumping in my chest.

Slowly we leaned forward and stared into the darkness.

Chapter Two

We saw a small, leathery creature. Its head was round and gnarled – like the knob on an ancient gatepost. Its body was barrel shaped. Its pointed ears sprouted great bushes of hair. Its nose was fat, its mouth wide. Its eyes were mouldy poached eggs – big, gloopy and horrible. It racketed about in the drain like a golf ball in a food blender. It tugged Zoom's line, cursing and spitting like a volcano.

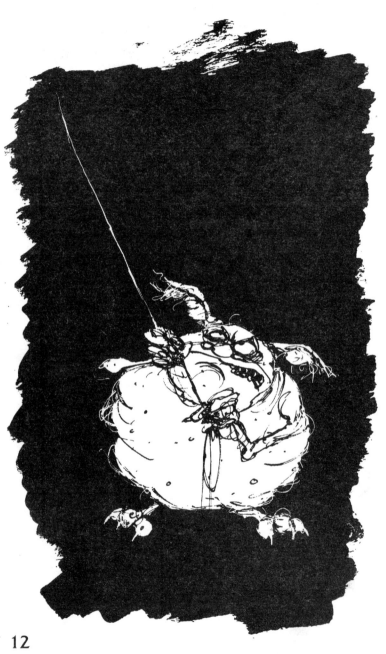

"Skredge it! Scrutt it! *Want it! WANT IT!*"

Zoom was so stunned she let go of the line. At once, the creature's eyes lit up. Now, I know we say that all the time without really meaning it, so I'll say it again more clearly: THE CREATURE'S EYES LIT UP. The drain was bathed in a green glow.

"Oh, wow…" Zoom breathed.

The creature held the line in triumph. "Yee-ess! Gottit! Now fish!"

Then it dived to the bottom of the shaft.

"Poor thing," Zoom said.

I stared at her. "*Poor thing*? It was horrible and it stole your crab-line."

"But it's hoping to catch fish," Zoom said.

"So?"

"So – it won't catch any down there, will it? Do you think it's hungry? I wonder what it lives on?"

"I wonder *what* it is," I said, "and *where* it's come from, and *what it's doing in a drain*?"

Three very good questions. Zoom ignored all of them.

"Never mind that," she said brandishing a squished bag of chocolate buttons. "Try these."

"But… what if it doesn't like chocolate?" I asked. "It wanted fish…"

Zoom stared. "*Not like chocolate?* Don't be silly."

We laid a trail by dropping bits of chocolate down the drain and scattering some on the ledge. We put some on the kerb to tempt it out. Then we waited.

"Gerritt-gerritt-gerritt… Mmmnn… Scrumpty!"

If a pig could talk, I thought, that's what it would sound like. Weird…

"Here it comes," Zoom whispered.

A skinny brown arm wriggled through the bars of the grid, and a bunch of bony fingers spidered towards the chocs on the kerb.

"Now!" Zoom shouted.

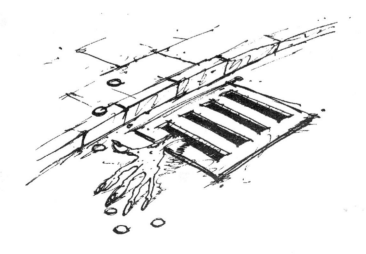

14

Chapter Three

We dived at it. I – Cheesy Adams, totally useless rugby player – threw myself into the gutter, with no thought for my personal safety. I grabbed that evil-looking arm and hung in there as if my life depended on it. Finally it stopped wriggling and lay limp.

"Let go, you idiot – that's me!"

Then I noticed that the arm I was holding was not long, brown and bony, but was wearing a pale blue jumper…

"Oops," I said. "Sorry, Zoom."

Zoom's other arm was down the grid. "I think I've got it," she said. "Help me drag it up."

It took ten minutes to wriggle the drain cover off without letting go of the creature, and another five to make it let go of the grid. It had long arms, stubby legs and a rough hairy body. It squinted in the sunlight and grumbled.

"Scrutt! Ppff… caught. Offitt!"

It hooked its bony hands into claws.

"Careful, Zoom," I warned.

"What, exactly, are you?" Zoom asked.

The creature glared, cracked its hairy knuckles and bared its pointed teeth. "Troll," it growled.

"I'm losing it," I muttered, "I thought it said *troll.*"

"Don't be such a wuss, Cheesy. It did say troll.
Well, it's not any animal we've ever seen, is it?
And it talks. If it *says* it's a troll, then maybe that's
because it *is* a troll."

"What now?" I asked.

"We'll take him home," Zoom decided.

"How?" He looked like the world's most evil
toddler. We'd never get him home without
attracting attention.

"Stuff him in your backpack," she said.

It was a struggle, but we did it. We had just
finished, when a huge bloke with tattooed arms
came out of the last house in the road and
scowled at us.

"Oi, you, get lost! We don't want kids hanging
around here. Clear off."

From the doorway another huge bloke called, "Leave 'em, Eric, they're 'armless."

"No, Arnie," Eric said. "They're not harmless – they've been messing with the drains."

"What?"

Arnie's expression changed. His eyes narrowed, his mouth grew meaner. He began to walk towards us. Then he started to run.

"Quick, Zoom, *zoom*!" I shouted, and we legged it like supersonic bats out of extra-hot hell.

Chapter Four

As we ran, the troll in my backpack bounced and giggled like a machine-gun with hiccups. When we finally stopped and gasped for breath, he stuck his ugly, mud-coloured head right out of the bag and yelled, "Again!"

Then he grinned.

"I wish he wouldn't do that," Zoom said.

"Yeah," I agreed. His grin was so wide you felt his head would fall in half!

"Will he give us three wishes?" I wondered.

"He's more likely to give us fleas," Zoom said. Then she went serious. "We should let him go," she said. "We've no right to keep him prisoner."

I knew she was right. I opened my bag. "OK, troll. You're free."

The troll snorted, folded his arms, and shuffled deeper into the bag. "Frogsnot stay puttit. Home."

He wanted to stay! Zoom was thrilled. But suddenly, I wasn't sure – would you want something called *Frogsnot* living in your backpack?

"Not comin' out. Nottit-nottit-nottit."

He had a very *so there* look in his eye and I had the sudden sinking feeling that arguing with Frogsnot would be even more useless than arguing with Zoom. I was snookered.

We took him home.

When I write my best-seller: *Cheesy's Monsters*, there will be a whole chapter about why you shouldn't keep a troll in your bedroom. Now I will just say: ANYONE WHO KEEPS A TROLL IN THEIR BEDROOM IS TOTALLY OUT OF THEIR TINY MIND!!!!

Here are three reasons:

1) They smell like dustbins ripening in the heat.

2) They have disgusting eating habits.

3) If they don't get their own way they go into mega-sulk. *Meltdown.* Nuclear wobbler. Believe me, a troll in a strop is a serious problem.

The instant my backpack hit the carpet, Frogsnot leapt out and shot under my bed. He started shredding my comics. It was total destruction.

"Stop! That's my *Beano* collection!"

"Makin' bed."

"Hold on," I said "I'll get you something else."

Mum had a pile of magazines by her bed. I grabbed some.

Frogsnot sniffed them, then scrunched them up. "Scratch-paper. Like brambles and thorns…"

A bramble bed – that sounded awful. "Would kitchen roll be better?" I asked, but Frogsnot was already asleep.

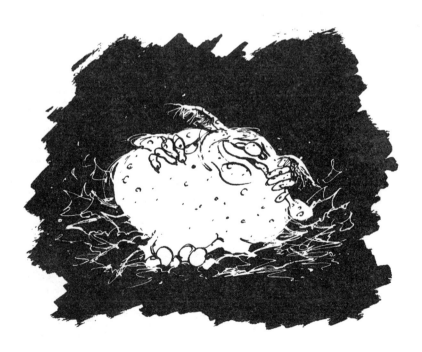

"Scratchit-thorns," he crooned softly. "Ded-cumptubble. Scritchety-scratchit… aah… Zzzzz…"

Trolls snore. And how! Imagine a rhino snorting. Now imagine a steam-engine chuffing up a hill. Mix the two and add a dragony hiss. Got it? Well, that's Frogsnot snoring. Still, a sleeping troll didn't need watching like a wide-awake one, so, I closed my bedroom door and went down for tea.

After tea we watched TV. There was a newsflash.

Thousands of fake banknotes had appeared in Westerby. The police believed the forgers were hiding out nearby.

The photo-fit showed a tough-looking man with mean eyes. He wore a black hat pulled down over his forehead.

"What a useless picture!" Dad said. "That hat covers half his face."

"It reminds me of somebody," I said.

But I couldn't think who.

Chapter Five

Have you ever tried sleeping while giant pigs snuffle under your bed? Me neither – but I'll bet a troll is noisier. I plugged my ears with screwed-up loo roll and, finally, I dozed off.

I was woken by the creepy feeling of a long, traily thing crawling *out* of my ear. This is truly terrible, because if it's crawling *out*, it must have crawled *in*… and has probably done something desperately horrible before leaving…

I opened my mouth to scream – and this revolting, hairy, bony finger slid on to my tongue. I spat and sat up.

Frogsnot was on my bed eating the loo roll from my ears.

"Gross!" Then I saw the clock – 2.00 a.m. "Go back to sleep!" I said.

" 'Ungry."

There was no point in arguing.

We crept downstairs. For such a noisy sleeper, Frogsnot was an amazingly quiet creeper. He moved as smoothly and silently as a drop of oil.

Softly, I closed the kitchen door behind us. "Sshh," I warned. "Don't wake Mum and Dad."

Frogsnot grinned. He ransacked the cupboards, rattling cans and chucking packets. He tossed cornflakes like confetti. Then – disaster! He found the fridge.

"Ooo – aah… oo-ah-oo-ah… oooo… mmmm."

Lit by fridge-light, his eyes gleamed with a soft, green glow. His grumpy frown was replaced by a drooly grin. He made jolly gurgling noises. His toes squirmed like happy worms. Then, he dived in.

Yoghurt pots flew like grenades. Ketchup squirted in red swirls. Frogsnot slurped and rummaged. Then he settled on the middle shelf, draped in slices of bacon, wuffling up great mouthfuls of runny French cheese. He wriggled and there was a noise like a welly in mud.

"Frogsnot," I whispered urgently. "You are sitting in a strawberry jelly!"

"Ah," he smiled. "Splurge-bum."

It was too much. I yanked him from the fridge, stuck him in the sink and turned the tap on.

"Eeech!" he yelled. "Nasssty water. Clean-up? *No*!"

"Go back to bed!" I said, firmly.

"Any fish?" he asked.

I tossed him a can of sardines and watched in relief as he slunk silently away. Then I looked round the kitchen and groaned.

The floor looked like one of those modern pictures where the artist has thrown paint at the canvas. The fridge looked like a hurricane had hit it. It took *hours* to clean.

Never again, I swore as I fell wearily into bed. From now on I'd take him rations. No more self-service in this house!

Next morning, when I went to school, I locked my bedroom door.

Chapter Six

Zoom grabbed me as soon as I arrived in the playground. I told her about the kitchen.

"What did your mum say?"

"She doesn't know – I cleared it up."

"She must've noticed there's food missing."

"She hasn't said anything."

But Zoom was right – I'd have to be careful what I gave to Frogsnot, I'd have to choose things that wouldn't be missed.

"I've brought my saved-up pocket money," Zoom said. "We'll buy his tea. What does he like?"

"Cheese and catfood. Bacon and jelly. Yoghurt and liver. Fish."

"We'll shop on the way home tonight," Zoom said.

School was normal and boring. Time passed like treacle, until finally the bell rang and Zoom and I legged it to the supermarket.

We bought cat food and pilchards and chocolate.

The checkout lady looked carefully at Zoom's five-pound note. Then she put it through a machine that shone purple light on to it.

"With all these forgeries about you can't be too careful," she said.

We walked along Ryman Road, and talked about our money being tested.

"Daft," I decided. "I mean, do we look like forgers?"

"Do we look like kids who've been shopping for a troll's tea?" Zoom asked.

We stopped at Frogsnot's grid and peered down. We weren't expecting to find another troll, but still, you never know... We never expected to find Frogsnot, did we?

"What's that?"

At the very bottom there was a nasty black blob.

Zoom sniffed. "Paint? No... not paint... but something like that."

36

From the corner of my eye, I glimpsed a large figure sneaking towards us. It was Eric. He looked very angry.

"*Zoom*, Zoom!" I shouted. We ran up Ryman Road like rocket-propelled ferrets.

For the second time in two days we collapsed in a heap on the waste ground.

"This is becoming a habit," I gasped.

Zoom was puzzled. "They were worried about us looking down drains yesterday. I thought it was to do with Frogsnot, but—"

"It's that black stuff, I'll bet," I said.

"Is it oil? Are they dumping waste?"

"I dunno," I shrugged. It didn't add up. Polluters dumped tonnes of stuff – not bucket-sized blobs. And they dumped it in rivers, not down drains. It didn't make sense.

Chapter Seven

Zoom came for tea. Afterwards Mum asked, "Cheesy, have you been giving the cat extra treats?"

"No." I held my breath. Was she on to me?

"Funny. There's all sorts of stuff missing from the fridge."

"Maybe you left a bag at the supermarket," I suggested. Then Zoom and I escaped to my room, threw ourselves on to the floor, and peered under the bed. Not a troll in sight.

"Frogsnot?" I called softly. Then I groaned, "Uh!" or maybe it was "Phuh!" or whatever noise you make when all the breath is knocked out of your body.

Frogsnot had thrown himself from the top of my wardrobe and landed on me as if I were a gym mat.

"Again?" he giggled.

"Oh ha-ha. Very funny. We've brought your supper. Not that you deserve it."

"Givusit."

"In a minute," I said. "I want to ask you something first."

Frogsnot's eggy eyes narrowed to slits. I'd better be quick, I thought, before he throws a mega-strop.

"How did you get here, Frogsnot? I mean, aren't trolls from Norway or somewhere?"

"Norfway. Norfmen. Fightkings! Frogsnot come in Fightkings' ship."

"*Fightkings*? Do you mean *Vikings*, Frogsnot?"

He nodded. "Dragon-ships. Fight."

Zoom and I thought about that. The Vikings were *history*.

"How old are you, Frogsnot?"

"More than 'undred man lives," he grinned.

"Wow, that's *old*."

"Frogsnot not old. Frogsnot *dancey*. Middle-troll."

"But how did you come to be in Ryman Road?"

In his funny grunty language, Frogsnot told us he'd lived in the drains since Ryman Road was built. Before that he'd lived in a cave in Westerby Hill.

"And before that?"

"Not sayin'." Frogsnot folded his arms, turned his head away and closed his eyes. "Frogsnot not tellin' any more. *'UNGRY!*"

"OK."

Frogsnot grabbed the catfood, ripped back the ring-pull, and stuck his face into the can. Then he ate the pilchards. "Fishy, fish-fish. Givusit. More-more."

He was about to rip Zoom's bag to bits, when he found the chocolate. He wolfed it and grinned. Then he did two enormous burps – one from each end, if you know what I mean.

"Ugh! Toxic!" Zoom held her nose in disgust.

"I'm being gassed!" I yelled and we escaped on to the landing.

Just before bed I suddenly remembered where I'd seen the face in the TV photo-fit. I rang Zoom.

"I think it's Eric," I said.

"There's only one way to be sure," Zoom said. "Tomorrow after school, we'll go to Ryman Road and look for evidence."

Chapter Eight

All next day time dragged by as if it was wearing lead boots. But, once 3.30 came, we were in fast forward. We whizzed round to Ryman Road like jets.

"You keep watch. I'll check the drain," Zoom said.

There was no sign of Eric or Arnie.

"Yes!" Zoom said suddenly. "This smell. It isn't paint, it's *ink*. Printers' ink."

She jumped up from the kerb and set off towards the house. "Let's get a look at the hide-out."

"Are you mad? What if Eric and Arnie—"

"Come on, Cheesy. Don't be a wuss."

We crept along the overgrown path towards the battered door. Suddenly Zoom stopped. "Sshh!" she said. "Listen."

There was a clacking sound. A whump-thump, clickety-splunkety sound. Definitely a machine.

"A printing press!" I said.

Zoom nodded. " You were right, Cheesy. And if we could get inside, we could prove Eric and Arnie are the forgers."

We talked to Frogsnot.

"Did you ever go inside the houses on Ryman Road?" I asked.

Frogsnot's expression grew even more cunning.

"Mightov. Mightov been 'ungry. Find somefink. Eatit."

"All the other houses in Ryman Road are empty," I said. "If you nicked food, it must have been from Eric's place."

"Frogsnot," Zoom wheedled, "if we give you some chocolate, will you take us in there?"

Frogsnot's eyes glowed an interesting shade of bad-egg green.

"Doglit… scrumpty," he whispered. Then he saw how much we wanted him to help us and his soppy chocolate-dream expression sharpened.

"Fish *and* doglit," he demanded. "Givusit. Now!"

Zoom handed over the chocolate nut bar. Frogsnot slid it inside the tuna sandwich and chomped. "Got rocks in it," he said, surprised and pleased. "Doglit, fish and rocks. Scrumpty."

"Yuk!" I said. "That is a gross-out. A total gross-out."

"OK, Frogsnot…" Zoom held open my back-pack, "…hop in! Take us to the Westerby Forgers!"

Chapter Nine

We crouched down by Eric's back gate.
Somewhere inside was proof that Eric and Arnie
were forgers, and we were going to find it.

Frogsnot climbed over the gate in seconds.
He unlocked it and we slid into the yard.

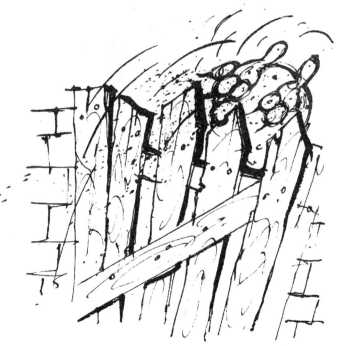

Frogsnot moved fast. He lifted the cellar hatch and disappeared inside.

Soon, the back door creaked open. Frogsnot pressed a skinny finger to his lips. "Sshh. Creepit." Then he beckoned and we ran across the yard and into Eric's den.

It was pitch black. The boarded windows let in no light. The smell of ink was overpowering. As our eyes adjusted to the dark, we saw a dim gold line of electric light shining underneath the door.

"OK," Zoom whispered. "Let's find out what's going on."

We stepped towards the door. There was a deafening crash and a yell.

"My leg!" Zoom sucked her teeth in pain.

Upstairs Arnie yelled. Then we heard the clatter of feet racing towards us.

"Quick!" I said. "Let's get out of—"

It was too late. The door swung open and light dazzled us. Zoom sprawled on the floor, tangled up with a set of tall wire shelves. Bits of paper floated around everywhere. Banknotes. The air was full of them.

Eric stood in the doorway, his eyes blazing mad. "Arnie!" he yelled. "Get down here. Fast!"

The banknotes drifted gently like giant snowflakes. We had found our proof, but would we ever get out of here to tell anyone about it?

Eric grabbed Zoom by the hair. Then Frogsnot attacked. With a blood-curdling howl, he sprang like a wildcat. His eyes burned green. He snarled. His teeth glittered like daggers. He was ferocious. Savage.

Eric didn't stand a chance. He dropped Zoom and backed off, protecting his face with his arms.

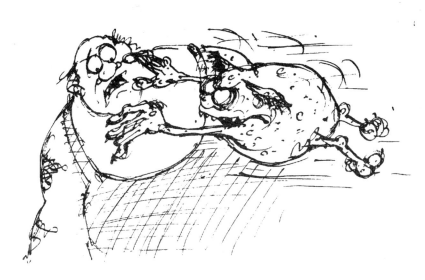

When Arnie arrived, Eric staggered into him. They went down like dominoes. Frogsnot roared and leapt at them. He was fighting mad – like a whirlwind released from a bottle.

Me and Zoom didn't hang around. We were out of there before you could say "Fightking".

At the waste ground we stopped.

"Did you see the money?" Zoom asked. "The ink on it was still wet. It's all the evidence we need." Then her face fell. We'd had to leave the evidence behind.

But printer's ink is sticky stuff, almost as good as glue.

"Nice one, Zoom," I said, as I peeled a newly forged fiver from the back of her T-shirt.

Chapter Ten

The police caught the forgers that night, and
Zoom and I made the front page of the local
paper.

There was a row, of course, about us tackling
dangerous criminals on our own. But Mum was
so pleased we were OK, and so proud of us,
that she didn't stay mad long.

The only problem was Frogsnot. He'd saved us
from Eric and Arnie and we were really grateful.
We wanted to thank him, but we couldn't.
Frogsnot had disappeared.

Finally we went back to Ryman Road. We dropped squares of chocolate down every grid.

Zoom giggled. "Anyone watching will think we're mad!"

"Not if we explain," I grinned. "If we tell them we're looking for a troll they'll *know* we're mad!"

At the last grid Zoom called softly, "Hello… Frogsnot… It's us…"

Nothing. Then we heard a weak, pathetic grunt. Frogsnot. He looked awful. He could barely crawl. We helped him up.

"Stink," Frogsnot mumbled.

Well, yes you do, I thought, but that wasn't what he meant.

"Poison stink. Eatit bad. Frogsnot sick."

Light dawned in Zoom's eyes. "I get it. Not *stink*. *Ink*. The ink in the drain made you ill."

"Listen, Frogsnot," I said. "You can't stay here. Bulldozers are coming to flatten the place."

So my bedroom became a troll sanctuary. The snoring was dire, the smell appalling. Mum refused to clean it.

"I'm not going in there until you've put all your dirty socks in the washing basket," she said firmly.

Then came the last straw. Frogsnot ate my goldfish. I heard a soft wet plop, a slippery swallowing noise, then a satisfied burp. The fish-tank was empty and Frogsnot was smiling.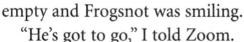

"He's got to go," I told Zoom.

"You can't just throw him out."

"You have him at your house, then."

She looked at me. "You're right," she said. "He's got to go."

But where?

"Norway. He could stow-away on a ferry."

"No dragon-ships!" Frogsnot shouted. "Sea storms rottin-horridbul. Frogsnot frow-up."

"We post him to Norway!"

"But the post goes by sea…"

We thought about him being sick inside a parcel.

"Maybe not, then," Zoom said wisely.

Then I had a brainwave. "The alley behind Cavendish Parade!"

"Cheesy," Zoom's face broke into a smile. "You are brilliant!"

"Yes, "I said, "I know."

Cavendish Parade has a chip shop next to a sweet shop. And as us experts know:

chocolate + fish = troll heaven.

So that's where we took him. He made his bed in a corner by the wheelie bins.

We visit him now and then, but not often in case somebody gets suspicious and starts to investigate.

Frogsnot is well and happy. We asked him once how many other trolls had come over with the Vikings.

" 'Undred. Maybees undred ana 'alf," he said.

Wow. Where are they all? My guess is – in places where you get fish and chocolate or jelly and bacon. That's where you should look. Don't believe that stuff about trolls turning to stone in sunlight. That's rubbish. Trolls wallow in slime and mud. Sunshine bakes them. They're not stone, they're just crusty. Believe me, I know about these things – I'm Cheesy Adams, Monster Specialist. See you around.

CATCH UP WITH CHEESY AND ZOOM IN:

BABYSITTING JELLYBLOB
Holidays are for fun. Relaxation.
That sort of thing.
But not this holiday. Cheesy and his best friend
Zoom hear a strange howling on the beach and
from then on things just get weirder and
weirder...

KRAXIS AND THE COW–JUICE SOUP
When Cheesy Adams and his best friend Zoom
see Kraxis's very hairy feet and very yellow toe-
nails, they know he is no ordinary tramp. Life for
Zoom and Cheesy goes ape. And for horrible
Arnold Spavin, it will never be the same again...

NEEDLEBELLY AND THE BULLY BOY
Kong Spong doesn't like Cheesy Adams and he
doesn't like Cheesy's best friend Zoom. School
camp looks like just the place to give them a hard
time, but Kong has reckoned
without Needlebelly, one of
Cheesy's monsters...

For further information about
Mega Stars please contact:
*The Sales Department,
Macdonald Young Books,
61 Western Road, Hove,
East Sussex BN3 1JD*